For Fergus Robert

First published 1986 by
Walker Books Ltd
184-192 Drummond Street
London NW1 3HP

First printed 1986
Reprinted 1986
Printed and bound by
L.E.G.O., Vicenza, Italy

British Library Cataloguing in Publication Data
Hughes, Shirley
Two shoes, new shoes. – (Nursery collection;6)
1. Clothing and dress – Juvenile literature
I. Title   II. Series
646'.3   GT518

ISBN 0-7445-0303-5

Two Shoes, New Shoes

Shirley Hughes

WALKER BOOKS
LONDON

Two shoes, new shoes,
Bright shiny blue shoes.

High-heeled ladies' shoes
For standing tall,

Button-up baby's shoes,
Soft and small.

Slippers, warm by the fire, lace-ups in the street.

Gloves are for hands and socks are for feet.

A crown in a cracker,

A hat with a feather,

Sun hats,

Fun hats,

Hats for bad weather.

A clean white T-shirt laid on the bed,

Two holes for arms...

And one for the head.

Zip up a zipper, button a coat,

A shoe for a bed, a hat for a boat.

Wearing it short...

And wearing it long,

Getting it right...

And getting it wrong.

Trailing finery, dressed for a ball

and into the bath wearing nothing at all!